OF HUMANS

(A collection of poems written from the perspective of an alien)

VESSEL

i

For,
The quiet ones.

CONTENTS

Part One
Of Humans;
Random findings

Part Two
Of Humans;
How They Love

Part Three
Of Humans;
Mental Health

Part Four
Of Humans;
Counsel

PART ONE; Of Humans

Random Findings

It is
Human Nature,
To appreciate
The Depths of Poetry, Sermon and Music.
Still,
They are inclined
To return
To Shallow Waters.
Wherein, They can splash around
As They please.
In which, They Believe
They run no risk of
Drowning.

Show me a human,

Who has everything.
And,
I'll show you a heart.
That wants
More.

All wars tell the same story,
Of how they are on their way to
Peace.

They grieve,

They mourn,
They move on.

Forgetting,
Is outside their reach.
Still, they stretch
All the same.

x

Good,

Resides in the human mind.
Evil, also.

The human mind is
A country,
And each opposing party
Campaigns for
Their vote.

They hold

Tradition,
In high esteem.

Even when they fall off
Its ladder,
And scrape their knees.

Every human,

Desires Greatness.
But,
Greatness is a colour.
And,
There are many
Shades.

The human mind,

Is a beautiful space.
But, too often
They crowd it with
Gaudy furniture.
Too often,
They have
Poor taste.

And,

When it comes to
Counting their blessings.
These humans,
Are all bad at
Math.

Envy,

**Is that shade of
Green.
That looks Good on
No One's skin.**

A symptom of believing only
In what you can see.
Is
Finding it hard
To believe in
Anything.

They say
Situations can change
In the blink of an eye.
Still,
I have seen situations convert
A blink of an eye,
Into a lifetime.

It is human nature,

To seek meaning.
In, every Tragedy.
But,
Tragedies
Rarely walk around with
Dictionaries.

T hey run to
Lies,
As a means of
Escape.
But,
Lies are
Roofless houses.
And, one day
It will rain.

Doubts,

Are powerful.
They not only demand
Humans look again,
They tell them
What to see.

How abstract humans,

Sound.
When they say
"These are dark times."
As though,
It isn't their hands
That paint
The times.

I have seen

Two unusual things shine so brightly,
The Sun gazes at them in envy.
Eyes,
That awaken to earthly Purpose.

The Smile
Of a human, who doesn't smile
Often.

Deceit,

Lurks around a smile.
Lingering,
Lurks around goodbye.

There are signs to know,
When a human is chasing after
The wrong thing.
The closer they get,
The satisfaction
Is less.
Should they find what it is they're seeking
There is no rest.
Tbey have to keep running
To keep it.

It is not uncommon,

For humans to think that
The road not taken.
Is filled with,
Bliss.
Yet,
In reality.
The road not taken
Is just another Path
With unfamiliar
Potholes.

Human,

When good things happen to you.
What is
The Vocabulary
Of your Heart?

A grateful heart
Uses words like
"blessed" and "loved"
An ungrateful heart,
Says
"coincidence"
"dumb luck."

When

Humans pray, with
Doubt
In mind,
Their Prayers,
Don't leave the room.
They hover,
Whispering confusedly
Amongst themselves
I hear them argue;
Left or right,
Which path to travel.
Above or beneath,
Where to go.

How Polite,

The past
Is.
To repeat
Herself,
When Humans do not
Hear her.
The first
Time.

To forgive,

**Is human.
To forget,
Divine.**

Doing
Good,
And
Being Good.
Are,
Two different things.
The former,
Is a shirt
Humans put on, take off.
The latter,
Is Their Skin.

Enlightened Ones,

**Do not
Wish upon
Stars.
They Know.
Stars,
Fall.**

"We are who we are"

Words,
Said by Humans,
Reluctant to change.

"We are who we choose to be."
Words that changes fate.

Everyone admits

To be in pursuit of
Happiness.
When they find it,
Few are certain of ownership.
It's a rare thing,
Hearing humans say
They're happy.
Usually, they say
They "Think" they're happy.

Dream,
But
Awaken.

Every Day,

Is a Gift.
Still, too often.
A Bad Mood
Bids Humans
Leave These
Gifts,
Unopened.

I have seen

Humans,
Call for
Change.
Only,
To bid her go
Home.
And return.
On a more convenient
Date.

Human Conscience,

Has Evolved.
There's
Right.
There's
Wrong.
There's Wrong done
With
Good Intentions.

W hen Humans look in

The Mirror,
They see either of two things.
What they are,
And.
What they've been told.
They shouldn't be.

A *human cliché*

"The storm will pass."
Odd comfort.
Time, ensures
The going and
Coming
Of things.
Not what they take with them
When they leave.

"No"

Is such a
Controversial word.
Clear, resounding
When uttered by human males.
By their females,
Low.
Muffled.
Sounds like Yes.

I am Distrustful,
Of their History Books.
They are
Heavy, with
The Proprietary Tone.
Of Humans, saying.
"It is
So."
When The Truth
Is simply,
"Yes or
No."

T hey are slow,
Hesitant.
When giving out
Trust.
You see,
They have come to equate
The speed at which it is given,
To
The speed at which it is taken back.

Wrong, sits on a shelf

At a high-end store.
It's price tag reads
£Guilt.00
And Humans are ever drawn
To items they can't afford.

To be
Believed,

Every Lie,
Disguises
Itself as
Truth.
But,
The Truth
Which comes as it is.
We accuse of
Plastic surgery.

Τhe Impossible,

Is accomplished.
Everyday.
By Humans,
Who call it by
A different
Name.

Every human,

**Deserves Redemption.
And,
Every Redemption
Deserves a human
That wants it.**

I have seen men,

Choose Violence.
Time,
After Time.
And, in turn.
I have seen Violence,
Choose them.

Too often,

They forget.
Failure,
Is just as temporary
As success.

T he struggle to do good,

Is gold.
The desire to do evil,
Is fire.
The latter too often
Melts the former.
Still,
That which is melted.
May yet harden
Again.

Never give a human,

The job
Of making you happy.
Some days,
They might call in
Sick.
Other days,
They might
Quit.

"Be Yourself"

Comes with
A clause.
If,
What you are.
Is accepted
By all.

Once upon a time,

Morality was worn with
Pride.
Now,
They hide it away from
Prying eyes.

Till date,

The two most tragic words
I've heard amongst humans,
Is
"Too late."

To Experience

Love and Hate,
Is not a Choice.
Humans, have.
They all must sip of both cups,
And then decide
Which will be
Their water.

I have seen

Two unusual things,
Shine so brightly
The sun gazes at them
In envy.
Eyes,
That awaken to earthly Purpose.
The Smile of a human,
Who doesn't smile often.

lvi

I do not believe,

Wisdom is a Treat
Reserved for the elderly.
For, I know
She knocks on the door
Of both Old and Young.
And, I have seen
The youths send her away
After reminding her of
Their age.

W alls,

Have ears.
The sun has seen it all.
Who says living has anything to do with
Breathing?
Add a little sadness,
And there's a switch.
Humans, exist.
While Things,
Live.

I have seen Apologies,

Travel down a road.
To and fro,
To and fro.
When they don't go with
The desire to
Change.

I used to think

That if a Human wasn't happy,
This meant they were sad.
But,
There are
A thousand emotions
Inbetween.
And, not enough
Facial expressions.
To go round.

Their obsession,
With Youth and Beauty.
Is obscene.
I have nightmares in which
History hands me a manuscript of
The things she's been writing.
The synopsis is.
Men,
Saved the world.
While, women
Stayed
Young.

Every Human,

Admits they want
The Truth.
Just not in all
Her Bright
Entirety.
They'd rather
She visit,
In dim shades of light.
That won't hurt
Their eyes.

And each day,

Human eyes dim toward
That great sleep called
Death .

But,
He who sleeps
Hopes to awaken
However sweet,
The dream.

When Happiness comes over,

Humans ask her where she's been,
They ask how long she's here for.
They ask if she intends staying longer
Than she did before.
They drive her away
With questions.

"Everything will be okay"
Are words I do not say.
For,
Things are never okay
For all,
And, I could never tell
The percentage to which a human belongs.
The percentage
On which the sun will shine on,
Or the percentage
To expect rainfall.

Amongst them,

I've come to find.
That brought to
Justice,
Rarely means
Punished.

Dual stages precede

**A human turning
Green,
With Envy.**

**Blue(s)
A stage of sadness
At another's success.**

**Yellow.
A bright sunny smile,
From pretending
They're happy for them.**

Sugarcoat-ing

The Truth,
Makes it easier
To swallow.

For The human
To whom it was prescribed,
And the problem,
That lurks inside.

To all who would follow,

The demands of Wisdom
Are unchanged.

One,
The promise
To use what she teaches
For Good.

Two,
The humility
To learn from scratch
What "Good" really
Is.

Simpler Times,

**Do not
Exist.
It is not above
Nostalgia
To mingle with
Deceit.**

Bad habits,

**Are never
Wrong.
When
Pleasure is
The Judge.**

Second Chances,

**Are filled
With humans,
Hoping for
A third.**

And, in a flash of insight

I caught a glimpse of
The perfect human life.
It had neither too much
Nor too little.

It had
Balance.

PART TWO; Of Humans
How They Love

lxxv

Tentative sips,

Precede
Greedy gulps.
This is how humans,
Consume love.

They invite

Love, over.
But,
When she comes with
Pain.
They,
Send them both
Away.

"**L**ove
**Will find
A Way."
Still,
Certain Humans tend to
Hold on
To their own
Map.
Just,
Incase.**

Humans,

Tend to listen to their hearts
When it is convenient.
When it says things
They want to hear,
They declare.
"It speaks."
When it says Things
They'd rather not hear,
They declare.
"It·beats."

● *A human cliché*

"If you love them,
Let them go."
A lie.
This is how
Little children
Lose
Their kites.

And once,

I saw two young lovers
Who thought.
The moments,
They shared.
Wouldn't run by so quickly
Like I knew it would.
It is
The silliness of Youth,
To trust
Time.

Together,

They were purple.
One day,
They felt
Whole.
The next day,
Split apart.
Into
Red and Blue.

Human Society

May have placed
A crown
On the head of
Lust.

Still,
It doesn't mean
She is of
Royal blood.

Love,

Is the only exception.
In which
When humans
Fall,
They aren't expected
To get back up.

When you have no money,

You're penniless.
When you have no love,
You're poor.

"This,
Thing.

You say
We have
Between us."

She told
Him.

"It,
Breathes."

Many love like

**The heathens do
All reverence and worship,
Till another deity
Comes along.**

And, what if

Clock-Hands place
Bets.
On just how long,
Two souls will stay
Apart,
This
Time?

You
Told her
You were Red,
And she was Blue.
It was how you
Justified
The Purple bruises
On her skin.

"Too Heavy."

The Ones who aren't right for you will
Retort.
When you give them
The World.

Humans,
Place such emphasis on
Love.

But,
Of what use is
An emphasis
If it's only spoken
In whispers?

Between each hesitation,

Every unspoken love declaration.

Humans, pair themselves
On a

Q
U
E
U
E

Waiting their turn
To blame
The stars.

Some days,

Are heavy.
Not meant
To be carried
Alone.

Ran out of time

Before they even began.
How long will
The Road not taken
Be starved of footprints?

Every human, preaches love.

**Few indeed,
Practice**

PART THREE; Of Humans
Mental Health

xcvii

Anxiety,

Speaks in the concerned tone
Of a friend.
Perhaps, this is why humans
Listen.
Perhaps,
This is why they don't recall
That in all her frantic presentations on
Negative outcomes,
None has graced reality with
Their presence.

Mental illness,
Is a terrorist.

Humans,
Are countries harassed by its
Bombings.
Pills,
Go in like a SWAT TEAM.
The therapist is Homeland,
Wanting to know things.
They oblige,
For if their bodies cannot sleep
How can their souls dream?

How cunning,

**Depression is.
Hiding behind a smile,
And
"I'm fine."**

c

Like sunset,

On days they wish would never end.
Melancholia brings with it
A loss of interest.

In reality,
Sunsets give way to sunrise.
But,
When humans listen closely
They swear they hear
The Sun say
She's retiring.

Pill-induced sleep,

Is different.
It doesn't quite know when to stop.
Spilling from night into daylight,
Head, aches worse than before.

Anxiety, is an

Imaginary friend.
Pointing nervously at unlikely events,
Telling humans what others
Think about them,
Never what they said.

Some,

**Find great comfort in
Prayers.
Pills,
Are futile.
Against ailments of
The soul.**

She locked the door, once.

She'll check again,
Twice.

OCD.

I have seen

A mirror, lie.
After it's been bribed by
The mind.

He was a bomb

About to go off

And all they did was

Mildly complain

About the beeping sounds

He made.

PART FOUR; Of Humans
Counsel

cix

Dreams,

Come true.
When eyes are not closed,
Dreaming.

CX

What you fear,

Fears something.
Find out
What it is.

There is no such thing as

"Little Acts of Kindness."

Every kind act,

Is grand.

Powerful.

Meant to take up

Space.

Every human,

Carries a heavy past.

But,
The good thing about
What can be carried,
Is that it can also be
Put down.

Do not look to

The stars,
For answers.
They blink,
They twinkle.
They say
"Yes."
They say
"No."
They guess.

What's lost may be found,

What's broken
May be fixed.
But,
What lives in denial
Of either of these.
Will remain
As it is.

Stand up for something.

Limited, is
The view
Of Those who
Sit.

Contentment,

**Is not the absence
Of wanting more.
It is
Being at peace,
When more doesn't
Come.**

Believing

**You know everything,
Ensures
You know nothing
New.**

Past lifetimes,
Should not concern you.
Any memory that succumbs
To being forgotten,
Is one you should not
Aspire
To repeat.

Temper,

Temper.
Such a waste of
Good flame.

What you fear,

Fears something.
Find out,
What it is.

Learning,

Is easy.
To Unlearn,
Is hard.

The former,
Is knowledge gained.

The latter,
Is knowledge gained
Recognized as
Loss.

Be careful,
Out there.
I've seen humans
Get shot.
For wearing
The wrong skin.

Hope,

Is a drug.
Get high.

The easy life,
Is a dream.

Human,
Awaken.

Sleep,

**Eludes the mind
That dares to
Dream.**

Those who feel
Life
Owes them,
Rarely get
Paid.

I have seen

Too many,
Give up
What suits them.
For the ill-fitting garment
Of trend.

A body,

That's healthy.
Beautiful,
Is.

O_{dd,}

**How humans who believe
In evolution,
Find it hard to accept that
People can change.**

Revenge,

May seem a fair deal.
Giving others a taste of
Their medicine.
Initially,
You may be sickened by your conscience.
With persistence,
You just might see it through
To the end.
But,
Satisfaction will run a few minutes late.
Then, she'll decide
She won't come.

Every vice,

Comes with an excuse.
A traumatic childhood,
Payback long overdue.

Still,
Consequences are known
To gaze long and hard
At each excuse,
And then mumble gravely.
"None will quite do."

Bruises of the mind,

Take longer to heal.

No colour update,
To inform on its progress.

Purple or brown,
You never know.

Some friendships last,

Yes.
But,
Many do not outlive
Their
Bracelets.

Things are rarely what they seem.

But,
Human eyes,
Are too easily
Convinced.

Freewill, is

A ticking bomb.
Yellow, black or red.
You don't know which wire to cut.
Realise,
You're always a decision away from
An explosion.

I have heard the creatives, say
"I am an artist. I need my pain."

I say.
Use your art
cure others' pain.

A problem ignored,
Has two outcomes.

The illusion,
That it is gone.
And,
The reality of one problem
Becoming more.

History, speaks ill

Of the dead.
When they've lived
Far from healthy
Lives.

The culture of

**Comparison
Is a plague.**

**Humans, must find
A cure.**

Human,

**You're a drug.
Someone's
Cure.**

Should a response,

Be neither
Yes or
No.
Deem it untrue.
Truth,
Is taciturn.
Lies, use up all the words
And seek more.

Regret, is a heavy thing

For a human to carry.
The more the excuse,
The heavier the burden.
Relief comes,
When you genuinely resolve
To do better
Than you did
Before.

The right thing to do,
Will rarely bring pleasure
To you.

It is bitter to
The tongue.
In the throat,
It burns.
But,
It is worth the wait.
The aftertaste.

Do not consider yourself

Rich in time.
For,
With abundance
Comes the Inclination
To waste things.

The brave,

Walk beside fear.
They know
She must witness them do
Those things she swore
They couldn't.

The right decision,

Will give you peace.
Above the din of people's opinions,
Above their criticism.

If there is calm in it.
However minute, however barely seen.
The right decision,
It is.

You all are not fools.

I know every addiction once promised you
Something good.

The gift of escape,
The gift of company,
The gift of forgetting.

Still, as time goes on
You'll find that
They lied.

cxlviii

Time,

Is not on your side.
She serves a higher purpose,
And bids you do
The same.

Both strong and weak,

May survive.
If neither
Take too seriously,
The titles of
"Strong" and "weak."

cl

What's yours,

Is yours.
If you're willing to work
Hard enough.

I've come to find

That if you break promises
One too many times,
You'll reach a stage
Where you'll know longer hear the noise it
makes
As it hits the ground.

clii

Driving loneliness away

With the company of
The wrong human,
Is like shooing ants away,
With Sugarcane.

F_{ear,}

Is a curtain.
Telling humans,
She's a door.

Walk through.

I've heard Humans say

They've changed.
While maintaining
The same company of friends.

The grass will always seem greener

In the fields of those who
Persist.

clvi

Many will tell you,
They've found God.
What they mean, is
They've found religion.

One aspect is filled with men
Declaring what God told them
Through visions and dreams.

The other,
Is hearing from Him
Yourself.

How to know a good poem?

What can I say.
A poem
That's any good,
Makes you feel like
It knows you.

"Too Heavy"

The ones who aren't right for you
Will Retort.

When
You give them
The world.

clix

Names are
Significant.

Why call
A "crush"
A crush.
If lust,
Isn't
Heavy?

clx

Too many,

Wield Religion like
A flag.
And, anyone can raise a flag.
Even though they aren't
Citizens,
Have never been
To its nation.

The wise,

Know when
A nation is burning.

They don't mistake
Its ash,
For snow.

Life's a journey,

Yes.
Still,
The locations you pick,
Are not always the destinations
You arrive at.

Be weary of peaceful smiles,
That cause riots
In a heart.

I have seen humans

Inquire of
Their purpose.
And, when they are told.
I have heard them
Ask again.

I have seen humans

Run from hurt,
And not get very far.

To all in search of

Happiness.
She is known to vacation in places
Where humans help
Each other.

Faith,

**To the onlooker
Seems a silly thing.
So does a weatherman
Predicting rain
On a sunny day.**

Today,

**Is disheartening
Doesn't mean
Tomorrow will be.**

**Human,
You must thrive more on
Hope
Than on
Oxygen.**

clxix

Happiness,

**Is
You and me.
Doing
The right thing.**

clxx

Self-doubt,

Speaks in the nicest of tones.

She never harshly says
"This won't turn out well."
She inquires politely,
"Are you sure it will?"

Do not be
Too hard on yourself.
Do not strip society,
Of its role.

There's an emptiness inside,
That humans try to fill with
Drinking, drugs and company.

And,
In moments of clarity
When they close their eyes
They see
That their efforts are shapes of
Triangles, square and rectangles.
While,
The emptiness inside is
A circle.

All avid followers

Of Trend,
Come to find.
That she who leads them.
Is just as lost
As they all are
That follow.

Lesser thoughts,

Must die.
For higher thoughts
To survive.
This is
The rule of survival
In the mind.

Feelings will

Come,
And feelings
Will go.
Indifferent to
Your yes
Or no.

Hypocrites

Adorn the first row.

Human,
Don't be among those
Who would rather not reap
What they have sown.

Do not allow

Mirrors,
Fool you.

Beauty
Does not always float on the surface.
Sometimes,

She deep swims.

Fate,

Is what you do with
Now.

W hen, how

I do not know.
But, if the bad comes
The good will,
Also.

clxxx

Every scar,

Tells a tale

Of how it

Healed.

And,

What if

The moon

Once criticised for shining too bright,

Gave up daylight

For night.

What if the stars blink at you,

Warning you of

Her mistake?

A heart of gold,

That others may try to

Steal

Is preferable to

A heart of stone

And all its

Security.

Giving is better

Than taking.

Nature's simple law.

For,

Giving is evidence of

Having.

Taking,

Evidence of loss.

clxxxiv

Y ou are tortured by

The words you do not say.

If life's a ghost story,

It is you

Who scares

Yourself.

Look in The Mirror

Long enough,
And you'll start to see flaws.

This is what happens when
You've been given the truth,
But you doubt and seek more.

clxxxvi

Two can keep a secret,

If neither wields

A pen.

Rules repel

The Heart.

Life,

Favours the bold.

Should the bold also be

Humble.

D_{eath,}

Is

A necessary thing.

And so is,

Living.

CXC

The human heart.

She lies.

A life devoted only to self,

Is one in close partnership
With death.

Work,

Without applause.

I have seen the best of works

Created in its absence.

The more layers

A human has,
The more fragile
The soul.

Humans who crave

The simple life,

Possess

The most complex of

Souls.

D o not envy

The birds and their wings,

As you watch them

Take flight.

When deep within,

You are terrified of heights.

To gain fame, and

Wealth.

Humans must scale through the stage

Of not wanting them.

Take care of Nature.

She's known to return

The favour.

ACKNOWLEDGEMENT

My sincere gratitude goes to my literary ally and sister, Dianah Ngamdy. Thank you for the long calls, and mutual brainstorming.
I am in awe of the Instagram and Mirakee writing community. Within months, I have bonded and learnt from the kindest humans, comprising of both writers and illustrators, who have shown support through their reposts, likes, and comments. Thank you.

cc

"You always write magic."

@samia.dilrus.writes

" I am extremely in awe of the depth of your writings… So offbeat from the rest stuff on IG, immensely appreciate. "

@poetic_cleopatra

"I don't know much of who you are… but your poetry is so special to me. I love every single one. I found you not too long ago, and I'm in love with your writing."

@saturnhousewriting

"@vessel_poetry You! Have become the singular reason I write something every day. Your consistency is amazing!"

@othyforyou

"Would love to see your writing seen by more people. You have the ability to take such complex emotions and situations, and in a few words express such incredible insight."

@poetlittlejack

cci

ccii

Made in the USA
Las Vegas, NV
01 January 2022

39893436R00121